Belle
the Birthday
Fairy

To Josie and Lucy, with love.

Special thanks
to Rachel Elliot

ORCHARD BOOKS
338 Euston Road, London NW1 3BH
Orchard Books Australia
Level 17/207 Kent Street, Sydney, NSW 2000
A Paperback Original

First published in 2010 by Orchard Books

HiT entertainment

A CIP catalogue record for this book is available
from the British Library.

ISBN 978 1 40830 810 3

7 9 10 8

Printed in the UK by Cox and Wyman

The paper and board used in this paperback are natural recyclable
products made from wood grown in sustainable forests. The
manufacturing processes conform to the environmental regulations
of the country of origin.

Orchard Books is a division of Hachette Children's Books,
an Hachette UK company.

www.hachette.co.uk

Belle
the Birthday
Fairy

by Daisy Meadows

ORCHARD BOOKS

www.rainbowmagic.co.uk

The
Fairyland
Palace

Fairy
Houses

Fields

Tippington
Town

Bakery

Birthdays come to everyone,
But getting older's not much fun!
Make birthday boys and girls feel bad.
Make them miserable and sad!

Banish presents, cakes and candles!
Turn their parties into scandals.
This year's birthday treat will be:
All birthdays filled with misery!

The Birthday Book

Contents

Parties in Peril!

"I can't wait to see Mum's face when she arrives at her surprise birthday party!" Rachel Walker said with a little skip of excitement.

"Yes, she'll be so amazed when she realises that you and your dad have arranged it all!" replied her best friend Kirsty Tate, swinging her rollerskates happily.

Kirsty was staying at Rachel's house in Tippington for the half-term break. Rachel's mum thought that Kirsty was just visiting for a holiday, but she was also there to attend Mrs Walker's surprise party!

"Everything's ready," said Rachel, counting the list off on her fingers. "The food, the music, the decorations for the village hall..."

"What about the cake?" Kirsty asked.

"Dad's ordered that from the baker's," said Rachel with a smile. "He's not very good at baking and he wanted it to be perfect!"

The friends were on their way to the
local park to go rollerskating. As they
passed the village hall where Mrs Walker's
party was to be held, Rachel squeezed
Kirsty's hand.

"Let's just quickly look inside," she said.
"I want to show you where I'm planning
to put all the decorations on the day of
the party."

"Ooh, yes!" said Kirsty eagerly. "I'm
really looking forward to helping you
decorate the hall and lay out the food."

They put their heads around the
door and their mouths fell open in
astonishment. A group of boys and girls
were there in their best party outfits, but
no one seemed to be having a good time.
The guests were talking in low voices and
they all looked upset. Some of the parents
were kneeling on the floor, clearing up
squashed cakes and spilled party snacks.
A box of decorations sat untouched
by the window. There was a stereo on

the stage, but it was making a strange whining sound and there was smoke coming out of it.

A little girl was standing by the door with her head hanging down. She was wearing a pretty pink dress with a white sash, but she looked very sad.

"Hello," said Rachel. "Is this your party?"

The little girl nodded her head and her big blue eyes filled up with tears.

"Everything's gone wrong!" she sobbed. "Half of the guests forgot it's my birthday today and didn't turn up. The food tables collapsed and squashed my birthday cake. None of the decorations would stay up on the walls. Now the stereo has broken so we can't even do any dancing."

Kirsty put her arm around the little girl's shaking shoulders. She didn't know what to say. The girl's mum hurried over to them.

"I'm sorry, Maya, but Dad can't mend the stereo. We're going to have to have the party at home."

"But we can't fit everyone into our house," said Maya, looking miserable.

"I know, but we have no choice," said her mum sadly. "You'll have to pick ten friends to bring with you. Everyone else will just have to go home."

Trying not to cry, Maya walked off with her mum. Rachel and Kirsty left the hall and carried on towards the park.

"I feel so sorry for Maya," said Rachel. "It's really unlucky that all those things went wrong."

They arrived in the park and sat down to put on their rollerskates. They both felt upset about the little girl's birthday being ruined.

"If only one of the Party Fairies had been here," Kirsty said with a sigh. "I'm sure they could have helped."

Rachel and Kirsty were good friends with the fairies, and had often helped them to outwit bad-tempered Jack Frost and his naughty goblin servants.

The girls stood up, wobbled a little and clung to each other for balance.

"It's ages since I've been rollerskating!" giggled Rachel. "I'm sure I'll be the first to fall over!"

A New Fairy Friend

Rachel and Kirsty had only been rollerskating for a few minutes when a group of older boys walked past carrying skateboards. Everyone looked fed up. Rachel spotted a boy who lived on her street among them.

"Hi, Sam!" she called. "Have you been skateboarding on the park ramp?"

"Only for about five minutes," said Sam. "It's Olly's birthday and we were planning a whole day of skateboarding. But the ramp collapsed and the park warden sent us home. It's the only ramp in Tippington, so it's spoiled all Olly's birthday plans."

"That's so unlucky!" said Rachel. "Two birthdays ruined in one day!"

Kirsty frowned as the boys walked away.

"It's more than unlucky," she said. "It's too much of a coincidence."

"You're right, Kirsty!" said a musical voice behind them.

The girls whirled around in surprise. The tall privet hedge behind them was sparkling with coloured lights, and sitting cross-legged on one of the leaves was a tiny fairy! She had long browny-blonde hair fixed up at one side with a purple flower, and was wearing a pretty purple mini dress with sparkly gold ballet pumps.

"Hi, girls," she said with a friendly smile. "I'm Belle the Birthday Fairy!"

"Hi, Belle!" said Rachel and Kirsty, stepping closer to the hedge so that passers-by wouldn't be able to see Belle.

"Is something wrong?" Kirsty asked. "We've seen two birthdays spoiled already this morning."

Belle's smile faded and she nodded sadly.

"King Oberon and Queen Titania sent me to ask for your help," she said anxiously. "There's no time to lose. Jack Frost has stolen the Birthday Charms!"

"What are the Birthday Charms?" Rachel asked in alarm.

"The Birthday Charms make sure that birthdays go smoothly in Fairyland and in the human world," Belle explained. "Now that Jack Frost has taken them and hidden them somewhere, birthdays everywhere are going horribly wrong!"

Rachel's hand flew to her mouth.

"Oh no!" she cried. "That means Mum's special surprise party on Saturday could be ruined!"

"Will you help me?" asked Belle. "Will you come with me to Fairyland and search for clues that might lead us to the Birthday Charms?"

"Of course!" cried Rachel and Kirsty together.

Belle fluttered above them and waved her wand. Immediately, a burst of purple and gold fairy dust erupted from the wand's tip. It showered down on the girls and they felt themselves shrinking to the same size as Belle. Beautiful gossamer wings appeared on their backs, and Rachel and Kirsty fluttered them in delight. It was a wonderful feeling!

Belle waved her wand again and this time the multicoloured sparkles spun around them in a dizzying circle.

"It's like a merry-go-round!" Kirsty

gasped, tightly squeezing her best friend's hand.

A few moments later, the colourful blur faded away and the girls were fluttering over Fairyland!

Goblin Intruders

"I thought we could start by flying over Fairyland and looking for clues," said Belle.

"So what are the Birthday Charms?" asked Kirsty, as they fluttered above the emerald-green hills, with tiny toadstool houses scattered around them. "What exactly are we looking for?"

"There are three Birthday Charms," said Belle. "There's the Birthday Book,

the Birthday Candle and the Birthday Present. The Birthday Book contains the details of everyone's birthdays in both the human world and Fairyland. Without it, nobody knows when *anyone's* birthday is!"

"No wonder half of Maya's guests didn't turn up," said Rachel, thoughtfully.

"The Birthday Candle makes all birthday cakes delicious, and grants birthday wishes," Belle went on.

"And the Birthday Present makes
sure that everyone receives the perfect
birthday gift."

"Oh, my goodness!" said Kirsty.
"Without those charms, nobody will ever
have a happy birthday again!"

"I think that's why Jack Frost stole
them," Belle said, nodding. "You see, it's
his birthday soon and he's feeling really
miserable about his age."

"So he wants everyone else to be
miserable as well?" Rachel guessed.
"How mean!"

"He doesn't want anyone to find out when his birthday is; not even the goblins," said Belle. "But without the Birthday Book, we won't know when anyone's birthday is!"

The three girls flew along, scanning the land below them. They were directly over the glittering towers of the magical Fairyland Palace when Kirsty gave a cry and pointed downwards.

"Look!" she exclaimed.

Far below them they could see three goblins scrambling up a ladder and climbing over the back wall of the palace! "I'm sure they're up to mischief!" said Belle. "Come on, let's go and find out what's going on!" Rachel, Kirsty and Belle zoomed after the goblins as they crept inside the palace through a back door. As the fairies entered the palace, they turned a corner and saw the goblins tiptoeing into the Palace Library.

33

"I'm going to give those naughty
goblins a piece of my mind!" exclaimed
Belle. "How dare they sneak into the
palace?"

She surged
forwards,
her cheeks
pink with
indignation,
but Kirsty
grabbed
her arm and
stopped her.
"Wait!" she
whispered. "What
if this has something to do with the
Birthday Charms? Let's creep in and
listen to what they're saying — it might
give us a clue."

Belle nodded and the three girls slipped silently into the warm, cosy library. The high walls were lined with books, some of them sparkling with magic, and in the middle of the room were six squashy armchairs. Beside each armchair was a round wooden table with a glowing lamp upon it.

"I don't think the goblins are here to do a bit of quiet reading," whispered Rachel as they ducked behind an armchair. "Look!"

The goblins were pulling books out of the shelves, row after row, and throwing them on the floor.

"Have you found it?" hissed the tallest goblin to the others.

"Not yet!" they replied.

"Well, hurry up!" the tall goblin told them. "If we can't find the Birthday

Book, we won't know when Jack Frost's birthday is, and we won't be able to plan his surprise party!"

Rachel, Kirsty and Belle stared at each other in amazement. The Birthday Book was hidden here in the Palace Library!

"It sounds as if the goblins want to find the Birthday Book as much as we do," Kirsty whispered. "Let's try and persuade them to help us!"

Belle looked doubtful.

"The goblins are never very helpful," she said.

"I think it's worth a try," said Rachel. "After all, they're disobeying Jack Frost by being here," she pointed out. "He doesn't want them to find the Birthday Book, so they must have a good reason for ignoring his orders. I think we should try to find out what it is!"

"Besides, it might take the three of us a long time to find the Birthday Book," agreed Kirsty, looking at the countless books that lined the walls. "We could use the goblins' help to search for it."

38

Belle agreed, so they stepped out from
behind the armchair and walked towards
the goblins, who were still busily pulling
books onto the floor. The girls tiptoed
up behind them...

Birthday Book Hunt

"It was a good idea of Jack Frost's to hide the Birthday Book here, wasn't it?" said Rachel in a loud voice.

The goblins whirled around in surprise.

"We would never have thought of looking here if it hadn't been for you goblins," Belle agreed. "We ought to thank you."

"Jack Frost knew that you silly fairies would never think to look under your own noses!" said the smallest goblin, sticking out his tongue. "Leave us alone!"

"Don't be so rude!" said Belle. "We want to help you."

"No way!" squeaked the goblins together.

"Listen to me, goblins," said Kirsty in a friendly voice. "We overheard what you said about throwing a surprise party for Jack Frost. You need that book as much as we do. How about making a deal with us?"

"What sort of a deal?" asked the tallest goblin suspiciously.

"You sneaked into the palace, and that's really naughty," said Kirsty. "We should really tell you to leave straightaway. So, here's the deal," continued Kirsty. "We'll let you stay and look up Jack Frost's birthday in the Birthday Book, if you promise to return it to Belle."

The goblins went into a little huddle.

The girls could hear them arguing in loud whispers. But after a few minutes they turned around and nodded.

"It's a deal!" they said in unison.
Then the great Birthday Book hunt began!
The goblins had no idea where in the library Jack Frost had hidden the book. The goblins searched the lower shelves, and the girls flew up to search the shelves that the goblins couldn't reach.

The hunt went on and on. Rachel's
arms were aching from pulling out each
heavy book to check it, and Kirsty's
wings were getting tired from hovering
in one position for so long. Belle kept
flitting down to the lower
shelves to magic back
the books that the
goblins were
throwing onto
the floor.
Outside the
tall library
windows,
the sun
began to set,
and they still
hadn't found the
Birthday Book.

"Are you absolutely sure that he hid it in here?" Kirsty asked as she reached the end of another row.

"Positive," said the middle goblin, wiping a few beads of sweat off his brow. "He said, 'Those pesky fairies will never guess that I've hidden the book in the Palace Library. I hope it makes them feel really uncomfortable!'"

"That's an odd thing to say," said Kirsty, fluttering to the ground to give her wings a rest.

Rachel flew down to join her.

"Perhaps we're looking in the wrong place," she said thoughtfully. "After all, Jack Frost didn't say that he had hidden the book on the shelves. He said that he wanted to make the fairies *uncomfortable*."

46

They all thought hard for a moment, and then Kirsty's eyes began to sparkle.

"What if he meant exactly that?" she said. "What if it's in one of the armchairs?"

The searchers stared at each other for a moment, and then each of them rushed to one of the six armchairs. They pulled up the seat cushions and the smallest goblin gave a yell of triumph.

"I've got it!"

Discoveries!

The little goblin waved a shining book
above his head, but he didn't have a very
good grip on it. The book flew through
the air and landed safely in Belle's arms.

"The Birthday Book!" she cried in
delight.

Rachel, Kirsty and the three goblins eagerly gathered around Belle. The Birthday Book was bound in gold, and when Belle opened it a puff of colourful fairy dust covered them all in sparkles.

"Look up Jack Frost's birthday!" cried the tallest goblin. "You promised!"

"A fairy always keeps her promises," said Belle calmly.

She turned the shimmering pages of the book. Hundreds of thousands of names were written there in tiny golden letters!

"There's my mum!" cried Rachel, pointing out Mrs Walker's name as the page turned.

"There's Jack Frost!" exclaimed the goblins at the same time.

"Oh, my goodness!" said Rachel, her eyes opening wide. "Mum's birthday is on exactly the same day as Jack Frost's!"

The goblins were delighted to have got the information they came for. They scurried home as fast as they could, after promising that they would never again sneak into the palace uninvited.

Belle hugged the Birthday Book to her chest and gave the girls a broad smile.

"I can't thank you enough for helping me find this!" she
said. "If it
hadn't been
for you
I would
have
thrown
those three
goblins
out of the
palace, and I
would never have
found out why they were here."

"I'm so glad we could help," said Kirsty warmly. "Does this mean that birthdays will begin to get back to normal?"

"I'm afraid not," said Belle, her smile fading. "People will remember the dates of birthdays, but without the Birthday Candle and the Birthday Present, things will keep going wrong."

"Then we'll just have to make sure that we find the other two Birthday Charms soon," said Rachel in a determined voice. "I'm not going to let Jack Frost ruin birthdays for everyone, and I'm certainly not going to let him spoil my mum's surprise party!"

"I agree!" said Kirsty. "Let's get started straightaway!"

But Belle shook her head.

"I have to return the Birthday Book to the present-wrapping room, where it's normally kept," she said. "Besides, look outside!"

Kirsty and Rachel turned to the library window. With all the excitement, they hadn't noticed that night had fallen in Fairyland. They could see the stars twinkling and the moon glowing.

"It's almost my bedtime!" said Belle, stifling a yawn. "And it's time that you two returned to the human world."

"Will we see you again soon so we can search for the other Birthday Charms?" Kirsty asked.

"Of course," said Belle with a smile. "Goodbye, girls... for now!"

She flicked her wand and there was a whoosh of colourful sparkles. The girls

closed their eyes.

When Kirsty and Rachel opened their eyes again, they were standing beside the privet hedge in the park, and the sun was shining. In the distance they could see Olly and his friends walking away with their skateboards under their arms.

"No time has passed at all," said Rachel wonderingly. "Oh Kirsty, I love magic!"

"Me too!" said Kirsty, hugging her friend. "Come on, let's do some rollerskating – and keep our eyes peeled for clues. Jack Frost could have hidden the other two Birthday Charms anywhere – and that includes the human world!"

The Birthday Candle

Contents

Cake Catastrophe

"I hope it stops raining in time for Mum's surprise birthday party on Saturday," said Rachel as she and Kirsty scurried along, huddling under an umbrella.

"Me too," Kirsty agreed. "Birthdays are never quite so much fun when it's raining."

"I wonder if Jack Frost has anything to do with this rain," said Rachel.

"I don't think we can blame him," Kirsty replied with a little giggle. "I think it's simply bad weather."

"I hope Belle is OK," said Rachel. "Time's running out for us to find her other two charms before Mum's party."

They had helped Belle the Birthday Fairy to find the Birthday Book that Jack Frost had stolen, but two of Belle's Birthday Charms were still missing. Without them, birthdays were going wrong all over Fairyland and in the human world. Rachel didn't want anyone's party to be spoiled, especially her mum's.

"Let's try not to worry," said Kirsty, putting her arm around her best friend's shoulders. "Queen Titania always says that we should let the magic come to us."

"That's true," Rachel replied, her face brightening. "Oooh, Kirsty, watch what you're doing with the umbrella! You just tipped water down my back!"

"Sorry!" said Kirsty, straightening the umbrella. "Look, we're here!"

The two girls had arrived at the bakery. Mr Walker had sent them on a special secret mission to collect the birthday cake that he had ordered for Rachel's mum.

"This window display always makes me feel hungry," said Rachel, pausing beside the glass.

"I've never seen so many yummy treats!" Kirsty agreed.

The shelves in the window were filled with a dazzling choice of cakes and pastries. There were pastries topped with fruit; cheesecakes shining with ruby-red strawberry glaze; and cakes heavy with sugared almonds and glistening silver balls.

The girls leaned closer to read some of the handwritten labels.

Kirsty let out a sigh filled with longing.

"They make the best cakes in the whole of Tippington," Rachel told her. "I can't wait to have a piece of the cake they've made for Mum."

"Let's go inside and see it!" said Kirsty.

Rachel stepped inside the shop. Kirsty shook off the umbrella and followed her in.

The bakery was full of wonderful smells, and Kirsty felt her stomach start to rumble. The warm scents of pastry, chocolate, nuts and cream filled the air.

"Hello," said Rachel to the jolly, plump baker behind the counter. "We've come to collect the birthday cake for Mrs Walker."

The man's smiling face fell. "Oh dear," he said. "I'm very sorry, but you're going to have to come back tomorrow instead. I'm having terrible trouble with that cake."

He pointed to the worktop behind him.
He had obviously been trying to ice a
cake, but there was something wrong.
The cake was misshapen,
and the icing was
sliding off. Sugared
decorations were
lying beside it. The
baker looked at
them with a worried
expression.

"This is the third cake I've
tried to make for Mrs Walker," he said.
"I've used the same recipe I use for all
birthday cakes, but it keeps going wrong.
The cake is coming out heavy and dry,
and the icing won't set. It's a nightmare!"

Rachel's eyes filled with tears, but
Kirsty tugged on her arm.

"We'll come back tomorrow," she told the baker. "Come on, Rachel."

"Why did we leave so quickly?" asked Rachel as they left the shop.

"Because of what I've just seen at the window!" Kirsty whispered urgently.

She pointed at three people who were crowding under one small umbrella and gazing at the cake display. Rachel rubbed her eyes and did a double take.

All three of them were wearing wellies, raincoats and rain hats. Between the top of the wellies and the bottom of the raincoats, she could see *green legs.*

"They're goblins!" she gasped.

Goblins in Tippington!

Rachel and Kirsty stared in amazement as the three goblins put down their umbrella and scurried into the bakery. They were all wearing wide-brimmed hats, and they spilled rainwater all over the bakery floor as they splashed inside.

73

"What are the goblins doing in Tippington?" Kirsty wondered aloud.

"I don't know," said Rachel, "but *we're* getting soaked! Put the umbrella up, quick!"

Kirsty raised the umbrella above their heads, but as she opened it something strange happened. The inside of the umbrella glowed with coloured lights like a disco ball...and then Belle spiralled down the handle, waving at them!

"Belle!" exclaimed Kirsty. "Thank goodness you're here! Three goblins have just gone into the bakery!"

"I know," said Belle, folding her arms. "I'm sure they're planning some mischief. I saw them creep out of Jack Frost's Ice Castle  at dawn, and they were acting very suspiciously, so I followed them. I'm glad to find you girls here – how did you know that the goblins were coming?"

"We didn't," Rachel explained. "We just happened to see them when we came to pick up the cake for my mum's surprise party."

"But something keeps going wrong with the recipe," said Kirsty. "The baker can't make it work."

Belle's face fell.

"I knew this would happen," she said with a sigh. "The Birthday Candle Charm helps all birthday cakes to form perfectly and grants the birthday person a wish. Until I find it, I'm afraid no birthday cakes are going to turn out well."

"Belle, could you turn us into fairies?" asked Kirsty. "We *must* find out what those goblins are up to."

"Good idea!" Belle said. "But I can't do magic here in the middle of the street."

"Let's go over there!" said Rachel, pointing to a little alleyway between the bakery and the shop next door.

The girls hurried down the alleyway
and stopped when they were sure that
no one could see them from the street.
Then Belle waved her wand and a flurry
of gold and purple fairy dust twinkled
around the girls. It was
like being caught in a
storm of sequins!
They giggled
happily as the
fairy dust
settled. They
had shrunk
to the same
size as Belle,
and their
gauzy wings
were glistening
with colour.

"Let's follow those goblins and find out what they're planning!" said Belle.

She zipped back up the alleyway with Rachel and Kirsty fluttering close behind her. The bakery door was ajar, and all three of them slipped in through the crack.

"Let's watch from the top of that display cabinet," said Rachel, pointing to a shelf. "No one will see us up there."

They fluttered up to the topmost shelf and sat on the edge. They could see the baker bringing out cake after cake to show the goblins. What on earth were they up to?

"These just aren't good enough!" squawked the tallest goblin.

"Load of rubbish!" squeaked the smallest goblin.

They were causing trouble already!

Kitchen Chaos

The baker had brought out all his most elaborate cakes and lined them up in front of the goblins. They weren't birthday cakes, so he hadn't had any trouble making them.

"Boring!" shouted the middle goblin, poking his bony finger into the first cake.

"Boring! Boring! Boring!" the other two yelled, poking their fingers into all the beautiful cakes in front of them.

"But this is my best selection!" cried the poor baker.

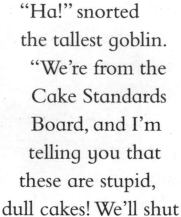

"Ha!" snorted the tallest goblin. "We're from the Cake Standards Board, and I'm telling you that these are stupid, dull cakes! We'll shut this bakery down unless you start making better ones!"

The baker rubbed his glowing forehead, looking upset.

"The Cake Standards Board?" he repeated. "But I've never heard—"

"We could make better cakes than this standing on our heads with our eyes shut!" yelled the middle goblin.

"Get out!" screeched the smallest goblin. "Come back in an hour and you'll see a truly magnificent cake!"

"I suppose I *could* take my lunch break now," the baker stammered. "It's been a difficult morning!"

"Go! Go! GO!" cried the middle goblin, pressing the baker's umbrella into his hands and shoving him towards the door.

The doorbell jangled as the baker left. The goblins locked the door behind him, sniggering.

"Those rude, nasty goblins!" cried Rachel, who had been watching in shock and horror. "How could they be so horrible to that nice baker?"

"And *why*?" Kirsty added. "What do they want?"

"Let's find out!" said Belle, fluttering into the air. "Look – they're heading into the kitchen at the back of the shop!"

The three girls flew through the colourful ribbon-curtain that separated the shop from the kitchen.

"Oh!" Belle gasped.

Suddenly, they were enveloped in a blinding white cloud!

"What is it?" gasped Kirsty, twirling around and trying to see what had happened.

"It's going in my mouth!" Rachel cried. "It's...it's...flour!"

"Fly upwards!" said Belle, coughing as she breathed in the flour dust. "As fast as you can!"

The three girls zoomed upwards, and their heads broke out of the floury cloud.

As the flour began to settle, they saw
that the three goblins were running
around the kitchen at top speed. They
had pulled off their enormous hats and
raincoats. The tallest of them had perched
a chef's hat on his head and the smallest
was wearing a striped apron. The middle
one seemed rather jealous and kept
trying to steal the others' outfits.

The goblins had overturned a huge
bag of flour, which had caused the cloud.
The floor was smeared with broken eggs,
dotted with spilled raisins and dusted with
icing sugar.

"Oh no!" Kirsty exclaimed. "They're
wrecking the kitchen. By the time the
baker gets back, everything will be
ruined!"

"We have to stop them," said Rachel with a determined expression on her face.

"Wait a minute," said Belle. "I don't think they're just here to make trouble. Look! I think they're trying to make a cake as well!"

The goblins had opened a cookery book, and were stirring lots of ingredients into a large mixing bowl.

"Stop shoving me!" squawked the goblin in the tall chef's hat. He elbowed the goblin in the apron and broke an egg over his head.

"It's my turn to stir!" wailed the middle goblin.

"Shut up and fetch the candle!" the tallest goblin snapped.

The middle goblin pulled a sulky face. He stomped over to the pile of hats and raincoats, and felt in the pockets. Then he pulled out a beautiful cake candle. It was a shimmering purple colour, and glittered magically in the light. Belle went pale and clasped her hands together.

"Girls, that's *it!*" she said in a breathless voice. "*That's* my Birthday Candle!"

Trapped!

As Rachel, Kirsty and Belle stared at the Birthday Candle in excitement, the other two goblins were still arguing.

"I'm the one with the chef's hat, so I'm in charge!" said the tallest goblin, shaking white powder into the bowl.

"Oh yeah?" snarled the one in the apron. "You can't be in charge – you don't even know how to read a recipe!"

He jabbed a green finger at the cookery book. "That says 'add *malt*', not 'add salt', you idiot!"

"Who are you calling an idiot?" shrieked the other.

They rolled across the bakery floor, grappling with each other, and crashed into the shelves. A colourful waterfall of cake decorations, ribbons, cake stands and candle holders rained down on them.

As they crashed around the floor,
the middle goblin continued
to follow the recipe.
Rachel saw him
add a large
spoonful of
chilli powder
to the mixture
and stir it in.

"That cake
is going to taste
horrible!" she said.
"They haven't even broken the eggs
properly – I can see bits of shell in there."

The goblin started to pour the mixture
into a cake tin, but he needed both
hands, so he put the candle down on the
worktop.

"Now's our chance!" Rachel whispered.

93

"I could zoom down and pick the candle up before he notices!"

"It's too dangerous!" gasped Belle. "The candle is right beside him. He'll catch you!"

Rachel gulped. She knew that it was dangerous, but she couldn't bear the thought of her mum's birthday cake being spoiled because of Jack Frost and the goblins.

"I've got to try," she said.

CRASH! BANG!

The other goblins were still fighting, and at that moment the middle goblin turned to put the cake tin in the oven. Rachel flew down to the worktop as fast as her wings could flutter, and Belle and Kirsty held their breath. Could she grab the candle before the goblin turned around again? Rachel reached the candle and put her arms around it, but it was too heavy! She couldn't lift herself and the candle out of the air, and the goblin was turning around!

Kirsty and Belle darted down to help
Rachel, but before they could reach her,
the goblin gave a yell of alarm.

"It's one of those pesky fairies!"

He grabbed a sieve and brought it
crashing upside down on top of Rachel.
She was trapped!

The other goblins dashed over to the
worktop. They were covered in egg,
flour and broken cake decorations, but
they grinned when they saw Rachel
hammering against the mesh of the sieve.

"Let me out!" she cried.

"Look, there are more of them!" squawked the middle goblin, pointing up to where Kirsty and Belle were hovering in the air.

"Aha!" shrieked the smallest goblin, capering around and blowing raspberries at them. "We've caught a fairy! We've caught a fairy!"

Belle put her hands on her hips.

"Goblins, give me the candle and let Rachel go right now!" she said in a loud voice.

97

"Shan't!" retorted the tallest goblin.

Kirsty frowned. She thought about the goblins creeping out of Jack Frost's Ice Castle.

"You're the same goblins who came looking for the Birthday Book, aren't you?" she said, thinking quickly. "Tell me, does Jack Frost know you're here?"

All three goblins went pale green.

"You're not going to tell him, are you?" asked the smallest goblin in a trembling voice.

Kirsty and Belle exchanged confused glances. Why were the goblins making mischief without orders from Jack Frost?

A Deal is Made

"Don't tell Jack Frost!" said the tallest goblin. "We want it to be a surprise!"

"This cake is for Jack Frost?" Rachel asked.

"Of course!" said the middle goblin. "We couldn't make it in the Ice Castle without him noticing."

"Now go away!" the smallest goblin squeaked.

"We're not leaving without Rachel and the Birthday Candle," Belle declared.

"That's our candle!" snapped the tallest goblin. "We found it down the side of Jack Frost's throne, so it's ours and we're keeping it!"

"They don't know that it's a magical candle!" Kirsty whispered quietly to Belle. "They just thought it would look good on the cake! They might give it to us in return for something better."

"What are you whispering about?" demanded the tallest goblin.

"We were just talking about the cake you made for Jack Frost's surprise party,"

102

Kirsty said. "Without magic it will take hours to cook. And the baker will be back soon and he won't be happy with the mess you've made. If you agree to help us, Belle can speed up the time it takes for your cake to cook and then you can head back to the Ice Castle!"

The goblins pulled faces at the idea of helping the fairies again, but Kirsty was hoping that their impatience would get the better of them.

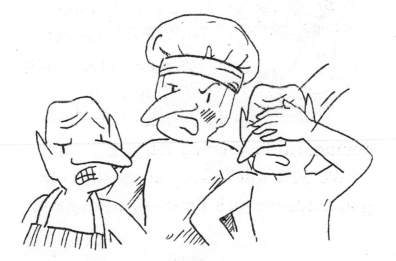

"If we agree, we could be back at the castle in time for lunch!" the tallest goblin whispered to the others.

That decided it! The greedy goblins nodded their agreement, and Kirsty smiled with relief. Belle waved her wand and a jet of gold and purple sparkles hit the oven. The door swung open and the finished cake floated out and landed on the table in front of the goblins. Everyone stared at it open-mouthed.

"It's horrible!" said Kirsty.

"It's spectacular!" gasped the goblins.

The cake was grey and had formed sharp spikes where the pieces of eggshell were sticking out of the mixture. It was misshapen and ugly...but it was *perfect* for Jack Frost.

"It *could* look even better with icing and decorations," said Kirsty, winking at Belle.

"Yes!" cried the goblins, clapping their hands and capering around the kitchen in excitement. "Make it better! Make it better!"

"I'll finish the cake for you — in return for two things," said Belle. "Release Rachel and give me the candle."

"Done!" the middle goblin declared.

He lifted the sieve and Rachel flew up to join Kirsty and Belle.

"Thank you, Belle!" she smiled, stretching out her wings. Belle flew down to the Birthday Candle. She picked it up and shrank it to its fairy size, and then she swept her wand over the cake.

Ribbons of blue and silver fairy dust began to curl around it. In a sparkle of magic it was transformed into Jack Frost's face, covered with silver- blue icing and topped with large candles. Belle had even written 'Happy Birthday' in silver balls on the side. "I'll carry it!" shouted the smallest goblin, making a lunge for the cake.

"No, *I'll* carry it – you're too clumsy!" yelled the middle goblin, picking up the cake and balancing it above his head.

He raced to the door, closely followed
by the other two, who were still
complaining loudly.

"They didn't even say thank you!" said
Kirsty, shaking her head at their rudeness.

"Never mind that," Belle replied. "I've
got the Birthday Candle back!"

"And the baker will be able to make
Mum's cake now," added Rachel with
a happy smile.

"That poor baker!" Kirsty gasped,
staring around at the mess the goblins
had caused.

"Don't worry!" said Belle, giving them
a wink.

She flicked her wand, and the whole
room shimmered. When the sparkles
faded, the kitchen was gleaming and tidy,
and a magnificent cake was sitting on the

worktop. It was decorated with pink icing
and a border of pink hearts.

"Perfect!" Rachel cried.

Outside in the alleyway, Belle returned
Rachel and Kirsty to their human size.

"I'm taking the Birthday Candle home to Fairyland straight away, but I'll see you again soon," she said. "Birthday cakes and wishes are safe – thanks to you two!"

She blew a kiss and disappeared in a flurry of fairy dust, and Rachel and Kirsty smiled at each other.

"Now there's only one Birthday Charm missing," said Rachel. "I just hope that we can find it before Mum's party!"

"I know we can do it," said Kirsty in a confident voice. "After all, if we can persuade the goblins to help us *twice*, we can do anything!"

The Birthday Present

Contents

Party Pooper

"SURPRISE!" everyone shouted.

"Oh my goodness!" exclaimed Mrs Walker.

Balloons flew into the air and party poppers banged all around the village hall, raining coloured streamers over the astonished Mrs Walker. Rachel and Kirsty each took one of her hands and led her into the centre of the hall.

"What a wonderful surprise!" gasped Mrs Walker. "However did you manage it?"

"I couldn't have done it without these two girls!" Mr Walker laughed, putting  his arms around Rachel and Kirsty. The guests crowded around Mrs Walker, hugging her and wishing her a happy birthday.

Three of Rachel's school friends went up to Mrs Walker. "Many happy returns!" said Alexandra, Tess and Nadia.

Rachel and Kirsty smiled at each other.

They had spent hours decorating the hall and laying out all the food. All the guests had arrived, and then at last Mrs Walker had walked in. She hadn't suspected a thing!

"Everything's going really well," Kirsty said in a low voice. "I was afraid that Jack Frost would spoil it because he's still got the Birthday Present."

"That reminds me – it's almost time to give Mum her special gift!" said Rachel in excitement. "Dad and I have bought her a beautiful jewellery box. I can't wait to see her face when she opens it!"

"Hi, Rachel!" called two girls from across the room. "Congratulations – it's a brilliant party!"

"Hi, Rosie! Hi, Natalia!" Rachel replied. "I'm glad you're enjoying it!"

"The cake looks gorgeous!" added a girl called Emma, whose dad had gone to school with Mrs Walker.

"I know – I can't wait to taste it!" Kirsty said with a grin.

Rachel and Kirsty helped Mr Walker
to carry the large present to Mrs Walker.
Mr Walker made a little speech, and then
everyone sang 'Happy Birthday'.

"How exciting!" exclaimed Mrs Walker.

She untied the big purple ribbon and
carefully undid the wrapping paper.
Rachel hopped from one foot to another,
feeling a bubble of
excitement rise up
inside her as
Mrs Walker
opened the
box...

"Oh," said
Mrs Walker.

"Oh, no!"
groaned Rachel
and Kirsty together.

There was no beautiful jewellery box inside the wrapping... just a pair of muddy old boots!

Mr Walker stared at the boots. He seemed to be lost for words.

"Well..." said Mrs Walker, blinking quickly, "these will be very useful for working in the garden. Thank you!"

But Rachel could see that her mum was upset. Frowning, she tugged on Kirsty's arm and led her away from the guests.

"It's not fair!" she whispered. "I know that Mum will enjoy her party no matter what presents she gets, but she would have loved that jewellery box!"

Kirsty nodded. "It must be—"

"Are you OK, Rachel?" called her friend Antonia, who had noticed Rachel's worried expression.

"I'm fine, thanks," said Rachel, giving her a smile.

She hurried determinedly towards the door and beckoned to Kirsty to follow her. She led the way outside and around to the back of the  hall, where weeds and tall brambles hid them from view.

"Ouch!" said Kirsty, as she brushed her hand against a stinging nettle. "Rachel, where are we going?"

Rachel turned to her with her hand on the magical locket around her neck. The King and Queen of Fairyland had given a locket to each of the girls. The pretty pendants were full of magic fairy dust, which Rachel and Kirsty could use to take them to Fairyland if ever they needed help from the fairies.

"We *must* help Belle find the Birthday Present – before anything else goes wrong at Mum's party!" Rachel said. "Kirsty, we're off to Fairyland!"

Party
Planners

The girls opened their lockets and
sprinkled the sparkling fairy dust
over their heads. Immediately they
were caught up in a swirling cloud of
sparkles. The glittering whirl swept them
off their feet and tumbled them through
the air.

As they somersaulted over and over,
Rachel and Kirsty felt themselves
shrinking to fairy-size. Then the sparkles
faded away, and the girls were standing
outside the glittering silver-and-pink
Fairyland Palace. The large doors were
wide open, and the girls could see that
the entrance hall was bustling
with activity. There were
tables laden with
food, dozens of frog
footmen carrying
boxes and
packages, and
a colourful whirl
of fairies flitting
to and fro.

"Oh, Rachel,
look!" Kirsty

exclaimed in delight. "There's Summer the Holiday Fairy! And the Rainbow Fairies are over there!"

Just then they saw Belle hovering in a corner. Rachel and Kirsty waved at her, and she flew quickly over to them.

"Hello, girls!" she said. "I didn't expect to see you here today."

Rachel quickly explained what had happened at her mum's party.

"What a mess!" exclaimed Belle. "Jack Frost has caused so many problems by stealing the Birthday Present.

T

He's even ruined his own surprise party!"

"What do you mean?" gasped Kirsty.

"When the king and queen heard that the goblins were planning a surprise birthday party for Jack Frost at the Ice Castle, they offered to help," Belle explained. "But there's a big problem. Follow me!"

She flitted through the palace towards the throne room, and the girls followed her, waving to all their good fairy friends as they went.

The king and queen were sitting on their thrones in the chamber. Rachel and Kirsty landed before them and curtsied.

"Welcome, girls!" said Queen Titania. "It's wonderful to see you!"

"It's lovely to be here again, Your Majesty," said Rachel breathlessly. "We came because something went wrong at my mum's surprise birthday party, and I'm sure it's because Jack Frost still has the Birthday Present."

"I agree," said the queen. "He's very vain, and he didn't want anyone to know that it's his birthday today! But we can't prepare the things we want to take to his birthday party until the final charm is safely back here, which means that the goblins are up at the Ice Castle doing all the work themselves."

"Things keep going wrong with the preparations," added King Oberon. "The food is burnt and the decorations have gone missing.

We have to try to get the Birthday Present back, but all the fairies are busy looking for the decorations and trying to fix the food. My magic has shown me that the Birthday Present is hidden in Jack Frost's Ice Castle, but I can't see exactly where."

"Let *us* go!" Rachel cried at once. "We could get inside the Ice Castle and hunt for the Birthday Present."

"Are you sure, girls?" asked the queen. "It could be dangerous!"

The girls looked at each other. The Ice Castle was a cold and scary place, but they had been there before and knew what to expect.

"We can't give up now," said Rachel.

"We want to do everything we can to help," Kirsty insisted.

"Very well," said the queen with a
grateful smile.

"May I go with them, Your Majesties?"
asked Belle.

"Certainly," said King Oberon. "But
remember, the goblins can't be trusted.
Look after each other!"

"We will!" said Belle, Rachel and
Kirsty together.

If they could find the Birthday Present,
Mrs Walker's birthday would be a
happy one and Jack Frost would get his
surprise party. But goblins guarded the
battlements, doors and windows. If the
girls and Belle were caught, they would
be in *big* trouble!

Inside the Ice Castle

Rachel, Belle and Kirsty gazed up at Jack Frost's home. The castle was built from sheets of ice, and it gleamed menacingly. The sky was thick with heavy, dark snow clouds. Goblins marched on sentry duty around the castle's pointed battlements.

"How are we going to get in," asked Rachel.

"Look!" cried Kirsty. A goblin was zooming along the road towards them on a motorbike, pulling a large trailer. He was wearing thick driving goggles, and a white silk scarf.

The girls darted behind a tree.

"What's in the trailer?" Rachel wondered aloud.

"I think it's party decorations!" said Kirsty.

A grey paper streamer had come loose and was trailing on the road. Just then, the goblin looked back and noticed it. He stopped the motorbike and jumped off to pack the streamer out of sight.

"That's our way in!" Kirsty declared in an excited whisper.

Belle, Rachel and Kirsty flitted over to
the trailer and tucked themselves under
the tarpaulin.

They couldn't see anything, but they
could hear the wheels of the trailer
rumbling over the icy, uneven road.
Then the engine was shut off and the
trailer was dragged over
bumpy cobblestones.

"Where are
we having the
party?" asked
a goblin
voice.

"In the
Great Hall,"
came the
reply. "Those
pesky fairies

haven't turned up to help, so we've got to do it ourselves! Jack Frost's presents are already in there. We'll decorate when he isn't looking."

The girls heard the goblins walk away. When their grumbles had faded into the distance, Kirsty carefully lifted the tarpaulin.

"All clear!" she said. They fluttered out of the trailer and looked around. They were in the castle courtyard, which had several dark corridors leading away from it.

JACK FROST

"Let's go!" whispered Rachel. "The goblins could come back any minute!"

The three friends flew into one of the corridors. It was narrow, cold and gloomy. At last they reached a pair of tall double doors with the words 'Great Hall' carved above them.

Suddenly the door handles started to turn. The girls looked around in panic. There was nowhere to hide!

"Up!" Belle whispered urgently.

They shot up to the ceiling and hovered there, pressing their backs against the cold roof. The doors burst open and Jack Frost stormed out.

He looked up and down the corridor.

"No one around for me to yell at!" he snarled. "Where are those stupid goblins?"

His long, thin fingers stroked his icy chin.

"I really hate birthdays!" he muttered to himself. "So I'm going to make everyone suffer!"

He strode off, his cloak flowing out behind him. As soon as he disappeared around the corner, the girls let out huge sighs of relief. They darted into the hall and closed the doors softly behind them. Jack Frost's throne stood in the centre, and long tables covered with grey tablecloths lined the room.

The three friends lifted the tablecloths and peered behind curtains, but all they found were cobwebs and woodlice.

"There's just one place we haven't looked," said Rachel.

Jack Frost's throne was standing on a raised platform. They searched down the sides of the throne and under the cushion. Then Rachel crouched down behind the throne. There was a hollow space inside the platform, and the three friends gasped when they saw what was inside.

"Presents!" said Kirsty in a breathless voice. "These must be the goblins' gifts for Jack Frost!" The girls pulled them out one by one.

"There's something else at the back,"
said Belle, peering into the darkness.

Rachel reached in, stretching her arm
as far as it would go. At last she pulled
out a little box, wrapped in shiny pink
paper and decorated with balloons.

"It's much sparklier than the others, and
it feels as light as a feather!" said Rachel,
wondering what this present could be.

Belle's eyes were shining with excitement.

"That's because it's the Birthday Present charm!" she said. "We've found it!"

A Brave Act

Suddenly the double doors were flung
open and the girls heard a host of
babbling voices. Kirsty peered around
the side of the throne.

"It's the goblins!" she exclaimed.
"They've come to decorate the hall for
the surprise party. Belle, can you magic
us back to the palace?"

Belle waved her wand, but nothing happened.

"Jack Frost must have put a spell on this room," she said in a worried whisper. "It means that I can't do magic until I get outside."

"We're trapped!" Rachel exclaimed.

"If we can't return the Birthday Present to the palace, the preparations for his party won't work," cried Belle.

"And it's only a matter of time before the goblins come around the back of the throne and spot us," added Kirsty.

She looked at her best friend in panic, but Rachel was gazing up at the tall, pointed windows of the Great Hall. One of them was slightly ajar, but there were three goblins standing right underneath it.

"We can't fly out of there," said Belle. "The goblins would be close enough to grab us."

"Not if they're distracted," said Rachel with a little smile.

"That's it!" Kirsty exclaimed. "Rachel and I will create a distraction on the other side of the hall. While the goblins are looking at us, you can fly out of the window!"

Belle looked worried.

"I don't want to leave you here," she said. "It could be dangerous. What if the goblins catch you? What if Jack Frost finds you?"

"The king and queen are coming here for the surprise party," said Rachel. "We can face anything when we know our friends are on their way!"

Belle hugged them both.

"I think you're both really brave," she said. "Thank you! I'll be as fast as I can!"

Rachel and Kirsty held hands and flew out from behind the throne, heading towards the far end of the hall.

"Hey, goblins, over here!" shouted Kirsty.

The goblins let out howls of anger.

"It's a pair of pesky fairies!"

"Get them!

"Catch them!"

"Stop them!"

The goblins all rushed to join in the chase and a sea of bony green fingers snatched at Rachel and Kirsty.

155

Not one of them noticed Belle slip quietly out of the window. Rachel and Kirsty saw her go, and smiled at each other. Now they just had to keep out of the goblins' way until help arrived!

The two friends flitted around the hall, dodging this way and that to keep out of the goblins' clutches. One goblin jumped

onto another's shoulders and tried to grab Rachel, but she did a somersault in midair. The goblin lost his balance and crashed to the floor with a yell.

Another goblin jumped up and down on the bouncy throne cushion and then launched himself through the air at Kirsty. She flew to one side at the last minute and the goblin hit the dangling chandelier and hung there, squealing for help. It was pandemonium!

"Just keep them busy!" Kirsty panted, flying higher to escape a particularly lanky goblin.

"My wings feel so tired," gasped Rachel. "I'm not sure how much longer I can—"

"WHAT IS GOING ON?" roared a furious voice.

The girls screamed, and all the goblins froze on the spot. Jack Frost was standing in the doorway!

"Fairies!" Jack Frost hissed. "I know why you're here! You'll never find the Birthday Present."

"You're too late!" said Kirsty.

"Shut up!" he snarled. "I hid the silly charm too well for you to find it!"

He lunged towards the throne.

"He'll find the presents!" squealed a goblin. "Stop him!"

Every single goblin hurled himself at
Jack Frost, who disappeared in a scrum
of green arms and legs.

"Get off me!" his muffled voice yelled.
"I'll banish you all, you stupid goblins!"

"That would be a terrible mistake,"
said the gentle voice of Queen Titania.
"They're only trying to give you a happy
birthday."

The fairies had arrived!

Parties Galore!

With a wave of the queen's wand, the Great Hall was transformed into a sparkling party scene. Fairies fluttered in carrying icy party food and frosted snowflake decorations. The grey tablecloths turned silvery-blue and the ceiling shimmered with glistening icicles.

The goblins scrambled to their feet and
rushed to add their decorations to the
room. Jack Frost stood up, scowling and
smoothing out his beard.

"What do *you* want?" he snapped.

King Oberon stepped forward.

"Everyone deserves a
very special birthday,
including you," he
said. "The goblins
care about you
and they wanted
you to have a
wonderful party.
We were happy
to help."

Jack Frost's eyes
opened very wide.
His mouth fell open.

"Getting older is something to be celebrated!" Queen Titania added.

Jack Frost looked too surprised to speak. Then the three goblins who had organised the party stepped proudly forward, carrying the misshapen cake. Its sharp, ugly spikes were frosted with blue-silver icing, and there were candles stuck out of it at all angles. Silver balls spelled out 'Happy Birthday!' across the bottom, and the goblins had added a grey ribbon as a finishing touch.

As Jack Frost stared at it, everyone started to sing.

"*Happy birthday to you!*
Happy birthday to you!
· *Happy birthday dear Jack Frost!*
Happy birthday to you!"

There was a moment of silence, and then Jack Frost leaned forward, closed his eyes and blew out all the candles.

"There's something missing from this party," he said.

"I hope he's not going to do anything mean," Rachel whispered.

He turned to a few of the goblins and tapped his wand on their heads...and they were transformed into the Gobolicious Band!

"Hurray!" shouted the goblins.

King Oberon gave a wave of his wand and a stage appeared.

"And now, a special performance from Frosty and his Gobolicious Band!" King Oberon announced with a smile.

Jack Frost pulled some sunglasses from his pocket and stepped up to the microphone.

"Maybe birthdays aren't so bad after all," he said. "Let's rock!"

It was the best party ever held in the Ice Castle. Rachel and Kirsty danced with all their fairy friends. They even tried to dance with the goblins, but the green creatures kept treading on their toes and giggling.

As night fell, the queen beckoned to Rachel, Kirsty and Belle.

"I am so grateful to you for finding the Birthday Charms," she said. "Thanks to you, we were able to show Jack Frost that birthdays *can* be fun."

"We were glad to help," said Rachel, hugging Belle.

"It's time that you were getting home," said the queen with a twinkle in her eyes. "I believe you have another party to attend!"

"My mum's birthday party!" said Rachel.

Belle hugged Rachel and Kirsty goodbye. "Thank you so much for all your help!" she said.

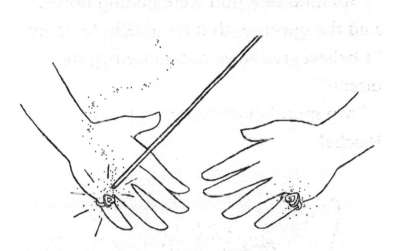

She tapped each of them on the hand with her wand, and there was a sparkling flash. When the girls looked down, each of them had a heart-shaped ring on her little finger.

"Thank you!" they gasped.

As they spoke, a whirl of glittering fairy dust surrounded them. They felt themselves rising into the air and spinning as if they were dancing.

When the sparkles faded, they were standing outside the Tippington village hall.

"Let's go and find Mum!" Rachel said eagerly.

They ran back into the hall, just in time to see Mrs Walker opening her beautiful jewellery box.

"I must have got the boxes mixed up!" Mr Walker was saying. "Silly me!"

"Thank goodness," said Kirsty. "It's the perfect present!"

Rachel smiled at Kirsty and squeezed her hand.

"No gift could be better than the adventure we've just had!" she said.

The Twilight Fairies

Now it's time for Kirsty and Rachel to
help the Twilight Fairies! The first fairy
they meet is

Ava the Sunset Fairy

Read on for an exclusive extract...

Strange
Sunset

"Look, Kirsty!" Rachel Walker said
excitedly to her best friend, Kirsty Tate.
It was a warm summer's evening, and the
girls were standing on the deck of a little
red and white ferry as it chugged its way
along a winding river. "I don't think we're
far from Camp Stargaze now."

Kirsty looked where Rachel was
pointing and saw a wooden sign on the
river bank. The sign was in the shape of
an arrow pointing downriver. It said 'This
way to Camp Stargaze'.

"Brilliant!" Kirsty beamed at Rachel.
"I'm really looking forward to this
holiday."

The girls and their parents were spending a week of the summer break together at Camp Stargaze. Kirsty and Rachel were thrilled because although they were best friends, they didn't live near each other. So they loved meeting up in their school holidays whenever they could.

"Not far to go now, girls," called Mr Walker, Rachel's dad. He was leaning on the boat rail with Mrs Walker and Mr and Mrs Tate, watching the beautiful countryside pass by. The river was surrounded by open fields and gently rolling hills, with green woodlands here and there.

"Oh, look, girls!" Mrs Tate exclaimed, gazing up at the sky. "The sun is setting. Isn't it lovely...?"

Win Rainbow Magic goodies!

There are five gifts in
Belle the Birthday Fairy and every one has
a secret letter in it. Find all five letters and rearrange
them to make a special birthday word, then send it to
us. Each month we will put the entries into a draw
and select one winner to receive a special birthday gift
from the fairies!

Send your entry on a postcard to Rainbow Magic
Belle Competition, Orchard Books, 338 Euston Road,
London NW1 3BH. Australian readers should write to
Hachette Children's Books, Level 17/207 Kent Street,
Sydney, NSW 2000.

New Zealand readers should write to Rainbow
Magic Competition, 4 Whetu Place, Mairangi Bay,
Auckland, NZ. Don't forget to include your name
and address. Only one entry per child.
Final draw: 31st May 2011.

Good luck!

Meet the
Twilight Fairies
in August 2010!

Ava the Sunset Fairy
978-1-40830-906-3

Lexi the Firefly Fairy
978-1-40830-907-0

Zara the Starlight Fairy
978-1-40830-908-7

Morgan the Midnight Fairy
978-1-40830-909-4

Yasmin the Night Owl Fairy
978-1-40830-910-0

Maisie the Moonbeam Fairy
978-1-40830-911-7

Sabrina the Sweet Dreams Fairy
978-1-40830-912-4